LOVE LOST IN TRANSIT

LOVE LOST IN TRANSIT

Devi Raghuvanshi

MyBooks Publication

First Published in November 2017

by

my Books
Think | Create | Publish

MyBooks Publication
publish@my-books.in

ISBN: 978-93-86474-41-4
eISBN: 978-93-86474-42-1

eBook & Cover Design
DigiConv Technologies

Dedicated to my Parents, who made me to read and write, while they were just the farmers.

This book is also dedicated to my friends all over who keep on reminding me when is my next book coming?

ABOUT THE AUTHOR

DEVI RAGHUVANSHI was born in Mathura, INDIA, the birth place of Lord Krishna and completed his Engineering Degree (B.E.) in Electrical Engineering. After working with big Corporates for 40 years, he ventured on a writing career.

This is his Sixth book an odd love and hate story,his first book "LOVE ON VENTILATOR", second book "LOVE TRIOLOGY, WHO TO COMPLAIN", third book "IT'S OK TO FALL IN LOVE AGAIN", fourth book "THE SON ROSE FROM THE WEST" and fifth book "MOHINI THE TIGRESS" have already been published.

DEVI RAGHUVANSHI lives in MUMBAI and he follows Sports as he himself has been a state level athlete.

He can be followed on www.facebook.com/ds.raghuvanshi.9 or www.deviraghuvanshi.com or Twitter @ Raghuvanshi_DS

ACKNOWLEDGEMENTS

I acknowledge and express my gratitude to my wife SUSHMA, for the input, spell check and all the inspiration and ideas, I conceived watching the degree of her patience.

My elder daughter PREETI deserves special mention for the emotional and financial support in bringing out the publication of this book.

I would like PAYAL, my younger daughter to be a partner in my this endeavour. Frankly speaking I have copied some of her blogs to make my book rich and true.

Finally I thank all my friends on Facebook, my college mates, for encouraging me to write this book. My heartfelt thanks, will not be complete unless I mention the big help I got from "Bhagvad Gita' and 'Google', the boss for anything.

You all are part of my these efforts BIG or SMALL.

DECLARATION

The contents of this book are wild imaginations of the author. Any resemblance of names, places or incidences are purely coincidental and unintentional.

The author does not take any responsibility for the loss or damage to anyone on account of publication of this book except he expresses his regrets for the damage if any.

DEVI RAGHUVANSHI

1

The human nature is to react to the circumstances. The author advises to provide a time lag of only five seconds to react and he knows that all impulsive decisions will be changed.

In his this book, "Sandra had taken all steps immediately and had suffered. Anil had also done the same. Evan had been an exception **SO DO THINK BEFORE YOU REACT**.

2

Sandra started a beauty parlour and SPA after her parents died in a car accident when she was just 19 years and a student at a hospitality and catering institute at Mumbai. It was some 1000 Sqft space in a very posh area of Mumbai Suburb which she named SANDRA'S PARLOUR, "Beauty with a Conscience". It was one of the best parlour and had a clear philosophy of beauty with a conscience. She had created a Salon that offered the best quality hair services which was natural and healthier for the present day environment. Her parlour had an interior tastefully done by using the recycled material, the floor was made of wood and walls etc. from green building concept of India.

She and her team were very proficient and qualified. Theyused to carry out high quality professional hair products esigned to ensure that the Clients look the best. The hair products, material were mostly eco-sensitive. No Ammonia was used anywhere even for colouring. She was offering full range of Salon treatment and styling services provided by her team of professionals, all in a clean air and centrally air-conditioned space. It was fully equipped for hair dressing, manicuring and other cosmetic treatment of women including bridal make-up or any service otherwise needed. In one corner of her parlour, there was space for SPA Salon which was different than the parlour. There was an individual approach to each Client. She had a special medical supervisor exclusively for SPA Salon who supervised the beneficial effect on a person as a whole unlike only on nails and hair. The difference between Sandra's Parlour & SPA was that her both parlour and SPA were equipped with professional equipments unlike any other parlour or SPA in the city.

Sandra's SPA was equipped for Pressure Therapy, Stone Therapy, Hippo Therapy, Ampelo Therapy, Aeroiono Therapy and Thalasso Therapy which nobody in the entire city had.

Her Clients included the brass from film fraternity, business and corporate houses and the visiting foreigners or tourists. She was doing a good business with peace of mind, with pride and far away from the scandals of this industry including massage parlours.

She was having a peaceful life of Euphoria, Tranquil and Serene.

3

Anil Malik was waiting to go for a business meeting next to Sandra's Parlour. The address for IT HUB NEW GENERATION was not traceable or visible. Anil needed help to locate the place. Right in front of him, was this gorgeous woman entering the SPA. The moment, Anil's eyes met, his stomach started doing FLIP-FLOPS. After introducing the way to IT HUB, the female entered the Parlour. She was Sandra, the owner of this beautiful Parlour and SPA. She even gave Anil few details of the head honcho of the IT Company as Sandra knew the wife of that IT Company Owner, being her Client. She also wished him luck for the success of his business meeting and walked away. Anil's meeting with the IT guys didn't materialize into any business dealing, but he surely got a kick in his mind for Sandra. He tried to find Sandra by wandering in that area and met a woman just outside the Parlour who enquired if Anil is lost. Anil said "No" and hurried for a cab to take him around the city and then to the international airport. Just as he was leaving, the receptionist from the Parlour called out for him and handed over a hand written note saying "Do not lose hopes, the world is too large to accommodate your genuine needs." Anil said to himself "Yes, I have lost the job but I did land the love, the inspiration of my life." He moved inside the Parlour and saw Sandra for the first time from a close distance.

For Anil, Sandra was the perfect combination of wit brain and beauty. She had well carved out features and big lotus eyes. She was an ultimate beauty, luminous perfection on the face and million dollar smile of Sandra made it difficult for almost all the males in and around that area to take their eyes off her. In all parties, Indian or Western, with her sensuous dancing moves and sizzling persona, she had been the heartthrob of so many people. Be it the crisp shirt and trouser or chic cotton saree, she was the most glamorous female. She used to carry each of her look very elegantly and gracefully. Even as business woman, she was simply beautiful, down to earth and elegant. Lastly the cute dimples, nice doe eyes, toned body and decent hair, made her the darling of one and all, favourite typically for fashion magazines.

Anil introduced himself . . .

Anil I am Anil Malik from Green Park, New Delhi. I am owner of a software development company having 10 employees. We are developing software for U.S. Companies as per their requirements like what I.T. Hub New Generation do. The only difference is that they are a major exporters of software to U.S. I had come here to request them to make some commercial arrangements so that they can off-load some of their business to us.

Sandra I am Sandra Fernandes, the owner of this small Parlour and SPA.

Anil Small? You are too modest. In fact when you directed me to IT HUB, this morning and the way you assisted me, I couldn't resist myself to go back to New Delhi without thanking you. More so when I received your hand written inspiring note, then it would have been stupid on my part to remain unmet and express my gratitude.

Sandra You are too cool a gentleman. Thanks for your thanks. If you need any other help, let me please know. How big is your company and what are your present, future goals and aspirations?

Anil was spontaneous, fun loving and live for the moment type.

Anil My turnover is Rs.75 Crores for last financial year. I would work hard to become the principal subsidiary of software giant Microsoft in India.

Sandra That would be a big achievement and would require real sweat and financial strength.

Anil Yes, I would do anything to raise the bar of my company's tech skills. If you permit me, may I also ask you the same question?

Sandra To be very frank, with you Anil, (I'll call you Anil, we are of almost same age) my company is biggest in Beauty and SPA products and services in Mumbai now. I would expect to have similar branches in all metro cities.

Anil That's inspiring and you would do it the way, you conduct yourself in your business, who all are helping you?

Sandra for a moment lost the focus and Anil noticed her wet eyes.

Sandra There is nobody in my family except a distant cousin who stays in Goa. I lost my parents in a car crash when I was just 19 years and was in final year of my three years hospitality course. I had no option but to stand on my feet and this was the area which I was fond of and studied in my college. My parents left some financial support so I started this Parlour from scratch. I am happy that I have proved to be a responsible daughter of my parents. I enjoy my work but they can't see it now.

Anil I am sorry Sandra. You have done an amazing task which no other woman could have done. I had also lost my father when I was in first year of my engineering. My mother was a teacher in junior college and she took the entire responsibility of bringing me up. After completing my degree course in engineering, I joined this very company as a trainee engineer and in next five years, I acquired this company and since then, I have been working 18 hours a day.

Sandra Oh, your efforts are no less. Your Mom must be super proud of you?

Anil She is my biggest asset, bigger than my company.

Sandra felt secured and protected with him as Anil was a very responsible sort of man. Sandra served him some nice hot coffee with cookies brought from Taj Cake shop. They both developed mutual respect and pleasure in making eye contacts. Anil left Mumbai but certainly left a deep impression like a promise to meet again and again.

After a week of Anil's departure from Mumbai, Sandra surely battled through the limbo between Anil being only a friend or potentially something more. "Does he like me or is it just my imagination?" "You seem to be 100 percent sure that he is seriously digging you?" she wasn't sure if he was ready to take things to the next level and commit to her exclusively. Just as she was in the turmoil of her thoughts, she got a text message from Anil which read something like this.

"Let us be grateful to the people and moments which make us happy, they are the charming gardens that make our souls blossom".

SANDRA, YOU ARE THE ONE

This became a daily routine not to forget, for Anil to send "Good Morning" each morning and "Good Night" every night to make Sandra understand that he remembered her throughout the day. Anil also remembered each and every minute details of Sandra's likes and dislikes. Sandra decided to know more of Anil. First time she only sent a big Smiley.

Sandra was invited as a guest speaker in an international conference at India Habitat Centre, New Delhi after 2 weeks. The subject of discussion was usage of green products. It was represented by people for close to ninety countries. It was a good opportunity to meet people and network.

Anil was in no way connected with this conference but he enrolled himself to be with Sandra. They spent this amazing last day at the conference venue hanging out and eating together and doing lot many things. It was really a perfect day.

Next day Anil invited Sandra at his place to meet his mother. Sandra thought that if Anil introduced her to his Mom, one thing that she could be sure of, would be that he loved her and felt proud of having Sandra as his girlfriend. Anil wanted Sandra to be introduced to his Mom as he wanted to seek her approval before approaching for next level. He also wanted to show Sandra how cool his mother was. He wanted to take the relationship seriously as there was a possibility that he was feeling a little insecure in the relationship and was not too sure of where it's heading from her side. He wanted to show his commitment in all possible ways. Sandra was pleasantly shocked but enjoying all moments. She never expressed it to Anil so openly ever before but her heart was beating on abnormal pace. She understood the seriousness of the situation.

Sandra met his mother the next day.

Anil Maa, she is Sandra, the one, I was talking to you always.

Mom Sandra, "I know you since he returned from Mumbai. He doesn't miss his breathe in talking about you continuously. How are you and how was your conference?"

Sandra I am good. Anil has made my conference more comfortable by attending it.

Anil Maa, did you like Sandra? She is a Christian girl.

Mom Does she have three eyes, four hands, five legs? Does she speak from her nose? She is a very sweet normal girl. You don't need to specify her Christianity.

Anil I told you that because couple of years back, you told me to marry anyone except Muslims, Christians or any other castes.

Mom It was two years back. Now I have no reservations and if Sandra agrees, I would love to see you both as husband and wife.

Sandra Aunty, we are talking a bit too early.

Mom I am cooking some typical North-Indian Punjabi food for you Sandra. Have your lunch and then go.

Anil Maa, No lunch today. I will take her around Delhi, show her Delhi and on way we will have our meals. You give her lunch and dinner, when she comes here again.

Mom Ok, Bye Sandra, Bye Anil.

4

Anil took Sandra in his car. Delhi is beautiful in the early morning, quiet roads, crisp air, milkmen and newspaper boys making their rounds, lively tea and breakfast joints, flower shops are at their best. The roads are wide and clean.

Lodhi Garden was the first stop for both Anil and Sandra, the place for morning walkers and joggers. It is a combination of Moughal and British culture. The garden was made by Moughals but was developed by Britishers as an area of beautiful, lush green garden dotted with medieval tombs, mosques and waterbodies. The landscaping designed, makes walking through Lodhi garden a unique experience. For Anil and Sandra, it was like a first date.

They then drove down to India Gate, President's house and Parliament Building and enjoyed the grand architecture, also enjoyed their drive through wide leafy avenues. The big shady trees were a treat to eyes. They now moved to Gurudwara Bangla Sahib, a serene Sikh temple. They also saw the prayers and sacred water tank and also the preparation for the LANGAR meal at the Gurudwara's voluntary community kitchen. One more important thing Anil shared with Sandra was that the big or biggest people of Delhi do shoe service for the devotees. Both of them covered their heads with a scarf as it is mandatory in all Gurudwaras.

Anil offered the best of non-vegetarian food at KAKE DI HATTI at CONNAUGHT PLACE. Sandra had never tasted such a tasteful of butter chicken in MUMBAI so far.

They reached a Qutub Complex which is UNESCO World Heritage site, a wonderful Moughal architecture and saw QutubMinar, a landmark of Delhi. They left early because they also wanted to visit AKSHARDHAM temple situated quite far off from Qutub Complex. It took them two hours to reach the place. It is one of the best place to see in Delhi. For Sandra, she really felt that it was a jaw dropping architecture, a fascinating fountain show. They both enjoyed boat ride and also the visit of huge garden.

Her return flight was at 10 PM from International Airport, New Delhi so they hurried to Janpath for some shopping. Anil gifted few artefacts as a momento of love and appreciation and dropped Sandra at the airport.

Sandra was always thinking that Anil after introducing her to his mother, expressing his feelings so freely, had already taken step to truly build a foundation with her. She came back to Mumbai but the couple kept in touch via Skype, Whatsapp and with a resolution to visit each other.

"Who do I share my joy? I don't have anybody. She called up her cousin sister in Goa and shared everything about Anil and Delhi."

5

Sandra was expecting the next move from Anil. Marriage proposals can be surprising or expected depending on the strength or equations of your relationship. Actually Sandra was certain of a significant proposal from Anil but she was restraining her excitement and she was not prepared to reveal to her friends until it was confirmed.

She had mentally prepared herself for the next step with Anil as she had assessed her life, career and relationship goals. She was aware of the maturity level and financial status of Anil so she wholeheartedly without doubts, was prepared to say yes to her marriage to him. On the other hand Anil had also done his soul searching before making such decision. He took a morning flight to Mumbai and fixed up with Sandra to meet for lunch at Retreat Resort Malad, Mumbai. Sandra this time picked him from Aiport and they both left in a car to reach Retreat. The drive from Airport to Marve beach through green cover of the road was giving them the hope of transformation of their lives. Both in their own way were thinking about this kind of commitment and were feeling excited, peaceful and anxious. Anil out of excitement or to show the mark of respect and love held Sandra's hand and she didn't try to take it off his grip.

They were sitting in one corner of the restaurant, lost in each other.

Anil "Yes, I have wanted to say that to you for so long, I can't think of anything, I want to do more, than spend the rest of my life with you." Would you marry me?

Sandra "Of course, I will. Did you ever doubt that? You have already become part of my life and now you are the love of my life. My answer to you is BIG YES." Though Sandra was all in agreement but since love had happened so quickly that she was not one hundred percent ready for. She said, "this was the most delicate situation, she faced."

Sandra "I have agreed to be your wife in principle but I have certain questions. We are based at two different locations. It would be necessary for one of us to relocate our work. Are you aware of and given it a thought Anil?"

Anil "I would relocate my office (Head office) to Mumbai and maintain a Satellite office in Delhi.

Sandra "I know that I care for you and you care for me very much and our relationship will really grow into something wonderful. Anil, I need a little more time as this is so sudden."

Anil "Agreed but not later than a month. I have brought two engagement rings."

Sandra Is it? "Anil, it is important for any couple to really discuss what they want out of life, place where they have to live, having children and their future, the importance of religion in our lives as we hail from two different religions and also our financial situations."

Anil "We have already discussed everything as you have asked. Regarding your religion, you are at liberty to follow any of our religions. For me Humanity is the biggest religion."

Sandra "Are you from this Planet or God has specially sent you for me? I am now ready to accept your ring and put the ring in your finger."

Anil placed his hand on his partner's hand and had shown some affection towards her. By this small gesture, Anil expressed and extended support and gave Sandra a sense of closure. He hugged her, kissed her and Sandra threw herself into his arms. They made this moment a very special one.

Now that both Anil and Sandra were engaged, they had to look forward for the wedding. Anil planned a lavish wedding and invited all his family friends and also included the names of all the guests which Sandra suggested from her side. They both sprang surprise to some of their friends. The date, venue and programme were finalized in Ashoka Hotel, New Delhi.

The marriage took place as scheduled in Hindu and Catholic systems and a big reception was hosted by Anil at Ashoka Hotel Lawns. They were now husband and wife. Some common friends arranged everything for a Honeymoon in Kerala. They both enjoyed their stay for 10 days in one of the most beautiful states of India. Kerala is God's own country and everything from its rich culture astounding natural beauty to the hospitality of its people. The couple also enjoyed the moonlit cruises down the backwaters of Kumarakom and Kottayam.

They returned to Delhi and after two weeks, both resumed their respective offices and also started the process of shifting Anil's Head office to Mumbai.

6

As husband and wife, there was excitement of a new romance. They both never allowed themselves to be accepted as a couple with routine and with a feeling that they have been taken for granted by each other. Anil asked Sandra everyday "How was your day?" He took Sandra every day for a walk after dinner. Sandra knew it very well that after dinner a walk makes their sex life great and Anil intended to hint at that.

Sandra made it a point to talk to Anil's Mom every day and visited her once a month for sure. This gesture on Sandra's part gave their relationship one more reinforcement. Though Anil was just a conventional husband but he did help Sandra in kitchen. He only knew how to make tea but at least he participated with Sandra as an assistant Chef. Sandra was a movie buff and Anil hardly saw ten movies in last twenty years but now he would book tickets for movies cultural shows including musical concerts online for Sandra and himself, would not use Computers at home and watch SaasBahu saga with his wife.

Sandra's clear communication always let Anil understand how much she loved him. Anil used to tell her that, " he remembered her throughout the day not only for her beauty but also for her talents and accomplishments. Sandy, you are now a wonderful woman who has changed my life and have made me so romantic." "What are you hinting at Anil? asked Sandra. You are a selfish guy but a darling too. You carry on, I will join you in half an hour in the bedroom, Sandra told him."

Time took a leap of one year. In past one year, they noticed that none of them even raised their voice or used unparliamentary words. They never criticized each other but supported and appreciated each other and complimented whenever opportunity gave them chance. Kissing Sandra on the neck and unexpected tight hug was Anil's weakness. Sometimes, he would appear from nowhere and start behaving like they were married one hour back. Sandra would meet his beloved husband's needs even when the time, ambience and the circumstances were adverse. But the man would not improve, "he would send a message saying how her eyes sparkle or how much I miss you. He would sometimes send flowers along with such messages." They were just perfect in both service and love.

One night when Anil came home from work, as out of his daily routine, he would kiss Sandra on her neck, Sandra made a TATTOO of an infant on her neck, "saying, don't hurt me, I am yet to be born daddy." Anil was over the moon excited. For him fatherhood was something, he had looked forward to for a long time. Sandra knew how would Anil react so she secretly filmed her husband's emotional reaction to the news that Sandra was pregnant. This film is a treasure with them till today.

Anil got some nice continental food and some spicy chicken from Taj Hotel. They both celebrated their this joy. Sandra called up Anil's MOM and told her that she would become a grandmother shortly. Anil's mother was on Cloud 9 and couldn't resist congratulating her son.

7

Anil's development of certain Software, had given him some international fame and many multinational companies were approaching for tie ups or take overs. Anil's this sense of adventure had become so overwhelming that he decided to finally take a plunge, work and live abroad. He needed to find a job, a tie up to enhance his image and earn a big money. To his good fortune, he got an opportunity to get associated with a big German Giant, the biggest in Europe.

He discussed with Sandra who immediately agreed with his proposition but the moment, she realized that he had to settle in Germany, she developed cold feet and hesitantly supported her husband to be known name like so many Indians working for major I.T. Companies. When asked about her moving to Germany with him, she expressed her inability due to her own expanded business of Parlours and SPAs. They agreed on arrangement of visiting each other 3 to 4 times a year.

Anil's new job required him to learn the German language and get more familiar with different cultural norms. He also discovered what skills were needed to make a good impression and be an asset to German company. He revived his old acquaintances with so many educational institutions and his former superiors to seek successful career aspirations. He collected all documentations that were needed to work in a new country like his university degree, financial statements from banks for getting a work permit. His company Infineon helped him with all relevant requirements of VISA etc. He first thought of a short term trip before the big move.

8

He joined Infineon as an associate. The company provided him nice accommodation and basic facilities. The apartment was cozy and was much cheaper than Paris, Canada or even Mumbai. Yes, the cost of living in big cities like Munich or Berlin was bit more higher. Food specially vegetarian was a bit of a problem but Asian cuisine was available in plenty. The cost of food was much less as compared to countries like U.S. and Canada. A good non-vegetarian food was easily available for 25 to 30 Euros per person. Groceries and day to day stuff was really cheap.

The country generally is peaceful and you would feel mental peace. There is no noisy traffic. Pollution is not heard, seen and smelt. Your privacy is guaranteed. The environment is really aesthetic and pleasing to live. Your lungs will get lot of pure and fresh air.

Anil's location was in Augsburg (close to Munich) which was basically for manufacturing chip card and security cards. Anil worked on the necessary Software to secure privacy of mobile phones, credit cards, I.D. cards and Computers. He soon became friendly. The German people are super friendly people. The ones that he met during his stay, were all open minded and well-travelled.

They opened their homes for him and introduced their families and took him out to great places. They spoke English in addition to their native language. He stayed in a small city of around 1,50,000 people, most of them could communicate in English. He did pick up German during his stay.

One in every seven workers originates from outside Germany. Almost 9 percent are Russians and Indians also have a significant presence.

Anil had few friendly neighbours. In six months, he became very popular with the families of Paul, Leon, Ben and Tim and started visiting them on weekends. They were all happy go lucky and party hoppers type.

On one such occasion, he was attending a party thrown by his these friends. There were few German good looking girls, one of whom he knew very well as she was working in his office so he had along conversation with. Her name was Laura. The discussion was mostly about their company, Infineon and they were engrossed in a long conversation. Laura was a pretty girl and surely a party freak. In between Anil wanted to go to the rest room and had to cross the people on the dance floor. Since the music was quite loud and people were not listening to him to give him way to move, so he tapped Hannah's shoulder lightly. Hannah couldn't hear him so he had to tap her shoulder. Hannah was the prettiest female present in the entire hall and the dance floor.

Hannah did not realize that Anil was standing right behind her trying to pass through. She only thought that this guy just wanted to dance with her so she turned around, saw him, lighted up in smile and hugged him. She carried him all over the dance floor. Anil was caught completely off-guard. He walked few steps of dance and after few minutes he headed to where he was urgently required to go. After he came back, he was introduced to Hannah by Laura. They then talked hours together on many topics like culture, India, Taj Mahal and respective families. Anil realized that German girls were friendly and open minded. What was important to Anil, was her personality, attitude and mutual respect.

The meetings between Anil and Hannah increased with passage of time. He asked her out for movies and dinners. She agreed to be his girlfriend, a good friend. Anil always wanted to know more and more about Hannah and he believed, "You'll never know if you never try." He was a little hesitant because of the colour of his skin which was not at all a factor in relationship and one would not feel that one colour was inferior to another.

Hannah, unlike German blonde, blue eyed and heavily built, was brown haired, tall radiant and beautiful as her internal beauty was shining out. Her beauty was described as a result of low cosmetic care the relaxation and rejuvenation of both body and soul. She was regular in her home SPA, a scented bath, facial treatment, foot massage, herbal tea and reading habits. She always wore casual outfit jeans and fashionable tops and would never compromise on comfort and fashion. Hannah was a fitness freak. She was very regular on jogging and swimming. She would most of the time leave her car at home and would take a bicycle with Anil for warm up exercises. She was an occasional drinker of bear with Anil. For Anil, she was a girlfriend and nothing more or nothing less.

9

Soon this liking changed to desiring. There was distinct change in their behaviour. They moved out of friendly zone to desire zone. Anil started having romantic fantasies for Hannah when they were both apart and whenever they were together, sparks used to fly between them. They both used to feel that their hearts were breathing faster when they saw each other or even by simply knowing that they would be meeting today. Each one of them couldn't wait to see each other. Anil always was trying to find excuses of meeting Hannah.

They used to have a routine friendly dinner once or twice a week but now a days, waiting for Tuesday nights was like a torture. Sometimes, they also actually felt that their relationship was platonic and had some longevity and depth but soon became a deeper romantic relationship. They both wanted it that way and they did it.

Hannah was a step further. She said to Anil, "the minute you have got sexual feelings towards me, a friend, it was that moment, turned more than just a friend." They both wanted to sleep together but said that "Being honest about your feelings, is necessary in all the relationships and in our instance truth telling is paramount failing which we would find ourselves giving each other a lot of mixed messages that could ruin our relationship. Coming clear on all issue is vital.

Anil was on a junction where he had to think about his life with Sandra, his legally wedded wife in India and his desirability of living with Hannah in Germany. Hannah was absolutely ignorant of Anil's marital status.

Anil thought to himself, "No one is above temptation. Everyone is flawed, while temptation differs from person to person, crossing the boundaries with someone other than your wife, appears to be one of the strongest. Yes it happens. Good people sometimes make very poor decision. However confession is best thing to do." In Anil's case it was two way confession, confession to Sandra, confession to Hannah as well.

Hannah was innocent. Anil was always under a guilt of exploiting Hannah. Understanding this very well that Hannah had a very strong character and a very strong head. It would not be possible to continue his relationship with her, the moment she came to know about Sandra. "Actually it was not only the temptation or lust for Hannah, but he deeply started loving Hannah and was almost sure of staying under one roof with her even if it would have costed him leaving Sandra.

He gathered guts and informed Hannah about his marital status with a kid.

The words from Hannah's mouth had escaped when he said. His that statement shattered every hope, she had nurtured about her life with Anil. Was it emotional infidelity? Hannah asked herself. She said to Anil, "I do not like to be called a woman of questionable ethics and moral standards who does not want a committed relationship or be called a BOMB level Babe who is good only in seducing and stealing married man from his wife.

She very clearly and firmly told Anil to clear his mess. "I am a Christian and would not hurt your wife. At the same time, I would not like to insult our relationship. I truly loved you Anil." Please take the decision after giving it a proper thought. I would, replied Anil.

10

Anil called up Sandra and informed her about his coming to Mumbai. It was a pleasant surprise and Sandra's heart knew no bound of joy. She was excited that she would meet her husband after one year. She was also excited that her son will also meet his father. She started preparation to welcome her husband. The entire house was cleaned and painted pink.

A warm welcome to Anil was planned. A large basket of fresh flower petals of different types to create a wonderful effect was ordered. Sandra chose only red coloured rose petals for the bedroom. The room was looking like a room for the newlywed couple, specially for the honeymoon. She also placed some old marriage pictures to make it more romantic. The entrance of the house was lit with coloured spot lights. She picked up the right kind of music to go with his creative welcome. Anil always preferred Bengali Rassogullas after dinner so Sandra ordered Bengal Sweets and some AmratsariNamkeens. The entrance door to the bedroom was having a poster, made by a famous artist/painter which read, "Welcome Papa".

Anil reached home as scheduled.

Sandra wore the dress which was the favourite outfit of Anil. Attraction was an essential component of a marriage or long time relationship. She took extra care for her physical and emotional self in order that her husband remained attracted to her. She wore a very attractive red dress as she knew that "men tend to be more attracted to women wearing red coloured dresses, Red evokes passionate feelings and emotions."

She appeared confident as confidence was an attractive quality. She was looking sexy, attractive and interesting.

"Every moment the very thought of his coming close to me or to know that I am going to meet my man after ages I get the butterflies in my stomach. Everyone has a different view and idea on what love means to them and those signs that you are falling in love again help you rejuvenate you mentally and more typically. I need my man tonight."

We had dinner together and went for a long drive in the city itself. He was quiet, only I was speaking. He did not speak a word about Germany, his job or anything else.

We returned home and went to sleep. I had lot of expectations from my husband speciallyafter we met an year ago. He slept an uncomfortable sleep. I tolerated this unmanly behaviour assuming that he could have been tired after all his flight from Frankfurt to Mumbai was almost eight hours or may be, he had Jetlag. I let of the things go and waited till morning to find out.

In the morning, when we were having morning tea, there wasn't anything unusual except I could notice dark circles below his both eyes. My first suspicious was that he had lost his job and he had undergone a tremendous physical and mental stress. I asked him what the reason for your low spirit and the marks below your eyes? Are you suffering some health problems?

He was not responding to direct questions. Upon coercing, he spoke with eyes looking down and not facing Sandra "When I talk to you now, my heart sinks deeper into shame and dishonor that is gone deep into my mind and skin. I feel like such a piece of garbage. No amount of physical pleasure or mental stimulation will compensate for the ridiculousness of my behaviour." I had fallen in a serious relationship with a German girl called Hannah. "Hannah is known to me since last one year, she is a colleague now, a simple beautiful dignified girl with a very strong character and virtues." Anil continued , " The most dangerous place for the marriage is work place. When two people who have a sexual attraction for each other work together, it's extremely difficult to control because of the repeated contact they have. If they work together, it is a recipe for disaster."

It all started on mutual liking which now had turned into desirability. I had started loving her unstoppably. Sandra heard him patiently and was numb and hopeless. For her Anil had admitted to have broken the bond of trust which forms the basic building block of a marriage or the committed relationship. She gave him a chance of relationship reversal from Hannah but was sure that no relationship would survive on continued duplicity and deceit.

She lost all the hope when she realized that Anil was neither honest with her and with himself nor he was willing to admit his mistake. Sandra was so far maintaining a bold posture. When it came to take responsibility, yes, he was sure that he would take the entire responsibility of Sandra and their son for life time. He was logically in no position to answer any of Sandra's questions but was firm and defiant in continuation of his relationship with Hannah.

Sandra almost reached a state of depression when Anil reconfirmed his affair with Hannah. His statement affected her mood, thought, behaviour, feelings and sense of wellbeing. She was sad, helpless, angry, ashamed and guilty for no reasons attributable to her. She asked Anil, "What is my fault? What is wrong with me that I cannot fulfill you or bewhat you want?"

Anil left the house, left Sandra & her son on whose mercy? Nobody knew. He reached Germany.

11

"A couple of months after he confessed to me, he suddenly stopped talking to me. I tried calling him repeatedly but he would neither pick up my calls nor respond to my text messages, I was beginning to worry and panic. What wrong I had done? Did he not love me anymore? He finally spoke to me one night. The tension in our conversation was tangible. I was so naïve, so idealistic, so stupid."

"I am not going to lie, it was pretty lonely. I cried myself to sleep some nights. I was still on hunt, I made a three months rule. Test period of three months was the last hope for Sandra for moving in life."

Three months also passed.

"Good relations never ask explanation because there is a silent understanding and a deep faith of unconditional love and trust exists in each other's life."

Sandra has already forgotten these statements so she went to Church, prayed talked to Church father and shut the door on Anil Malik forever.

She consulted doctors for some medical assistance for her depression. She started exercises as per the advice of her doctor who told her that exercises increase neuroplasticity of your brains and release neuro-chemicals called Endorphins which help to elevate your mood. The doctor also advised her to follow these rules.

1. Just get out of the house for a walk
2. Play some games to catch up with your son
3. Meet your friends
4. Don't isolate yourself
5. Go for shows, movies and musical concerts
6. As laughing is the best medicine, so see funny videos

He further advised Sandra to develop positive thought for a purpose.

She started doing everything as advised and decided to take care of herself, her son with a determination that she only will take care and raise her son on her own strength without depending on any help from Anil.

12

Exactly after two weeks, Anil got a glimpse of Hannah on a jogging track early morning. She was looking like a fairy in while black pants and dark blue canvass shoes. She was shining and her moon resembling round face was radiating early sunlight. Anil ran towards her as if he generated some robotic energy within his nerves. Since the day he met her last before going to India, he didn't remember even a single moment when he had not thought about her. For a moment, Anil kept glaring at her oceanic pretty eyes and next moment his head went blank. His heartbeats went way too louder and mouth started drying up. Anil tried to calm himself down and spoke few words but Anil was demoralized.

He asked Hannah if she had time to talk. How could she not have time for the person, she loved the most? Hannah asked him How he was and why he grew so thin? Why was he sporting this huge ugly beard? Why were these dark circles below his eyes? To which he cried and said "I miss you". They both cried that day. They walked and talked how miserable their these two weeks had been.

With great grief in her heart, she asked Anil, as what all was done in Mumbai and what was his decision for Sandra? "I have left that relationship back home and the marriage unofficially had been terminated.

Hannah informed Anil that Polygamy is banned in Germany. It is currently punishable by up to three years in prison. No one who comes here has the right to place their cultural entrenchment or religious thinking over the laws against individuals being married to more than one person at a time but they have quietly allowed polygamous relationship to exist. The immigrants who drive in Germany after marrying multiple wives in their home countries may be tolerated by legal authorities in practice.

She also informed Anil that the German authorities are known to be difficult and slow when it comes to marriage between German and other nationals. She suggested that it is far better that we plan to marry in Denmark or Las-Vegas and then getting a foreign marriage acknowledged in Germany is far easier than marrying here. But in case, you want to get married in Germany, Anil you would need to submit some documents. The couples planning to get married in Germany should start with the legal formalities as soon as possible. Minimum time expected is six months and could be early if luck favours you. The first place to contact is Embassy or Consulate and a local Registrar office. The most needed document would be a birth certificate, a passport stamped with proof of residence and proof that a previous marriage has been permanently terminated. You would also need a Health Certificate.

Anil was partly disappointed after he heard Hannah explaining the requirement and the attitude of German authorities. He informed her that he had all the certificates except a certificate that he was single from the Indian Court which seemed vital. He also informed Hannah with a heavy heart that there was no possibility also for getting that certificate. He asked Hannah whether there were other avenues to explore?

Hannah was understanding his predicament and his inability to do anything. Hannah suggested three options,

1. They try for normal German marriage
2. They get married in Denmark or Las-Vegas
3. They go for cohabitation which is an arrangement where two people who are not married, live together. Such arrangements have become increasingly common in western countries during past few decades. They often involve a romantic relationship and/or sexual intimate relationship on a long term or permanent basic.

Anil saw a ray of hope. Hannah further said that if her parents agreed or not, "we would have enough money to be happy in our lives. We decided not to bother and screw the world and come back together."

Hannah said, "Though I feel so sad and disappointed for Sandra but your basic statement that you would support her and the kid, has assured me of your good heart and humanity. I would also support Sandra and your son with you.

They then started staying together in live in relationship.

13

Sandra to herself, "The only thing worse than loving a person who doesn't love you, is remembering him and his memories." Anil was hurting her even now. Anil was selfish beyond words. She says, "I have lost what I loved and the whole world now looks like my enemy." Sandra concluded that there is light at the end of the tunnel and eventually felt better for having taken that step of forgetting Anil rather than continuing in a situation.

She always kept in mind, "Don't presume that it is better to carry on with the failing relationship in order to protect your child. If you cannot mend your relationship, it may be best to move on because children now a days sense what is going on.............. Time heals everything and as you got used to the new you. You searched love in Anil and now let love search you.

Tragedy doesn't come alone. While Sandra was undergoing such a big turmoil of life because of Anil, her finance manager Mr.Narayandid not deposit and file Income Tax returns and Service Tax returns and he misappropriated the money. The amount which was supposed to be paid to Service Tax and Income Tax Departments,was syphoned off to his personal account. The Service Tax department had sent a notice to attach the properties of THE BEAUTY PARLOUR & SPA for a default payment of Rs. 4 Crores including basic tax, interest on basic and penalty on that. They had sent the notice earlier which was not responded either by Sandra or her Accounts Manager. Based on information from Service Tax department, Income Tax deparment also served the notice. This department also cracked the whip on tax default by invoking its power to arrest and prosecute the evaders. To her good fortunes, Govt. of India opened an Amnesty Scheme vide which Sandra could have paid this tax with a penalty of 30 percent to avoid legal complications including arrest.

In the process after selling six of her parlours, she paid Four Crores to Service Tax department and Rupees One Crore to Income Tax department. Now she was left with only one parlour at Khar, Mumbai to supplement her basic needs. She also lost a large chunk of her customers.

Though it was a big loss but this gave her an extra energy and spirit to fight the odds. By now she had already become an iron lady with grit and determination.

14

They preferred cohabitation as an alternative to marriage because it was not possible to marry due to legal complications and due to objection by Hannah's parents for inter-religions relationship. They decided to get married later once all problems were sorted out. They also decided not to have children born out of wed-lock and concentrate in raising Evan, the son of Sandra and Anil.

Both Hannah and Anil had great understanding of the factor of stable and lasting relationship. Their interpersonal relationship was strong, deep like close association of acquaintance between two people. Their need to belong to each other was so deep rooted that they always felt a need to love and being loved sexual and non-sexual. Both Anil and Hannah were dominant and submissive depending upon emotional stress and the need of time. They were having relationship satisfaction which was flourishing, budding, blooming and blossoming. Hannah proved that she would be a better wife, economical wife, loving and caring wife. Now she was one of the best friends, Anil had so far. They both had the capacity for romantic love which had given them the depth of relationship; this had brought them close to each other physically and emotionally as well. Their main bond was due to the attraction to each other and initiation to maintain warmth of the relationship and then sustaining it further. They used to appreciate each other. Hannah was more matured than Anil so at times, she used to treat him with kid gloves and care.

Their intimate relationship was a mixture of friendship, platonic love, romantic love and sexual activity. Both Hannah and Anil were sexually very active and compatible to each other.

As professionals, they were doing very well.

15

It was almost three years since Anil left Sandra and Mumbai and close to one year of cohabitation with Hannah. Nothing specific was happening. It was Sunday afternoon when Hannah and Anil were sitting in the open courtyard of their house and were having beer before a late lunch.

Hannah Anil, "I would like to speak to Sandra today, there is no agenda but I just thought of her and Evan."

Anil "Why do you want to be insulted and scolded?"

Hannah "I don't think, this will happen, however if it happens, it's Ok. For me as we both are responsible for her this indifferent attitude. But I would speak to her now."

Anil connected Sandra. Sandra was about to sleep. Evan had already slept by now.

Sandra Hello, "This is Sandra Malik who is speaking please?"

Hannah "Hi, Sandra, this is Hannah from Germany. Can I speak to you for a moment if it is convenient to you."

Sandra "Hi, Hannah, what a surprise! How are you?"

Hannah "I am good, How are you and little Evan?"

Sandra "We are good too." How is Anil by the way?"

Hannah "He too is fine doing his bit."

I am sorry Sandra for the mess in your life but trust me. Firstly I didn't know that Anil is married with a son, secondly by the time I came to know the reality, it was a bit too late. Though I tried to explain to Anil to forget his this small and short relationship and go back to you but somehow in spite of his striving hard, he couldn't succeed and even I could not part with him. He loved me, I loved him and believe me, there wasn't any sexual orientation between us till that time.

Sandra "Yeah, Anil has told me everything how and when it started? How he couldn't reconcile with me and himself. Anil is a nice person and he has a kid/ baby in him. I have pardoned him because he loved you more than he loved me."

Hannah "Yeah, he is like that only."

Sandra Anil had told me, "He is thankful to you for sticking by him throughout everything. He also told me that you have worked hard throughout the years and stuck by him when he had essentially, absolutely nothing, you both have been together through thick and thin. He says, he owes her his success. His career would likely have turned out very differently if it wasn't you. You drive him to Gym and you also listen to all his dreams.

Hannah "That's partially true but he hadn't told you that he had never detached with you and Evan."

Sandra Then why haven't you married by now?

Hannah In Germany, you can't marry till your first marriage is fully terminated and the court in India issues a certificate to the person saying that he is single now.

Sandra "Please ask Anil to apply for divorce, I will sign immediately."

Hannah "I would not like to do it now and I have two conditions. (1) Both you and Anil will remain the closest possible friends. (2) You would also accept a special request not from Anil but from me."

Sandra "What is that?"

Hannah "I would tell you once you promise me that you would accept and respect it."

Sandra Hannah, you are such a sweet person and a much better human being so in all probability, I would accept it provided it doesn't interfere with my self-respect."

Hannah "I would like to, not Anil, would love to take total responsibility of Evan right from his schooling till he is professionally established and becomes independent."

Sandra "Hesitantly agrees to Hannah."

Hannah If you trust me, if you love me, I would also make one more request to you. We all meet either in Germany or India once a year without fail.

Sandra "You have won over me. Now I can understand how Anil must have lost him to you. I love you, I respect you and from now onwards, Anil is a free man without any guilt."

16

Hannah wanted Evan to go to the best school in India so she and Anil searched on internet 10 best Schools in India. Anil suggested some boarding Schools in Dehradun and Panchgani and also some Military Schools (SAINIK SCHOOLS) but Hannah didn't agree and wanted Evan to study in a co-ed Schools. According to Hannah the discrimination between boys and girls, the gender gap is minimized and the personal growth of the child is enhanced by virtue of the competition. Anil had no option but to accept her arguments.

Hannah had already discussed with Sandra and they both agreed to Evan in a residential school either in Dehradun or Panchgani when he becomes five years old. Laurence School Sanawar, was one more option available to them. When the question is about finding the best boarding school located in Panchgani, then the selection becomes tough. Panchgani is an education hub, there are several boarding schools. Hannah concentrated on these schools;

1. St. Peter's School, Panchgani
2. Sherwood School, Panchgani
3. New ERA School, Panchgani

4. Laurence School, Sanawar

After going to all these details, Hannah came to know that these schools admit kids from 6th Standard onwards. She was disappointed but never left the hope. She along with Anil searched another good School in Mumbai. Bombay Scottish School, Mahim, MUMBAI. This School was established in 1847 by Scottish Colony people for orphans which subsequently became one of best 10 Schools in India. This was chosen by Hannah after knowing the School syllabus which was affiliated with ISCE, New Delhi Curriculum and the School allumini consisted of people like Amir Khan, AbhisekBachhan, Rohan Gavaskar, Neeraja Bhanot. Hannah used the influence of German Consulate, paid Rupees Four Lacs and admitted Evan in Senior KG.

She was very happy for whatever she had done and more than Hannah and Anil Sandra was feeling happy and proud for her son being admitted in the prestigious School.

Hannah did it but never forgot that the next School for Evan would be Laurence School Sanawar as and when he becomes 10 or 11 years.

17

Hannah called Sandra after two weeks to find out her well-being and also about the School activities of Evan. Sandra told her that they were good and the kid is getting used to School activities. Sandra also informed her that Anil would be required in the family court to file for divorce by mutual consent. So you both should visit me in Mumbai so we could meet also. Hannah, "I would like to see you in person to ensure that you are more deserving than me for Anil." No, I am just joking. You are a wonderful female and also we have promised to meet each other once a year."

Hannah confirmed her commitment to Sandra and said, "I will ask Anil to arrange tickets etc. for both of us." We would be staying with you."

As scheduled Hannah and Anil reached Mumbai after a month. Sandra welcomed them with a warm welcome and open heart. She did Aarti to Hannah as per Indian customs for a guest who visited for the first time. She was comfortable with both Anil and Hannah.

After two days, they both filed for divorce and mutual consent. They both had a common advocate to process the system. The honourable Judge heard them and advised both of them to request the court for divorce after six months. This is the normal system as many couple during these six months, just reverse their decision for separation. It was only a matter of time. Sandra had mixed feelings after submission of the application for divorce. They were filled with wide range of emotions. She was feeling excited about her new anticipated freedom and at the same time, the next moment mourning the expected loss of life, she used to have. She knew that separation and divorce was an emotional process. She was happy that she could call her ex-spouse first in crisis. Being sad when a marriage ends is natural.

She was calm and composed as she had already passed a stage of acceptance and she accepted it with dignity. There wasn't any feeling of guilt and shame. There wasn't any fear and anxiety. Both Hannah and Anil now were the natural part of her support system.

Anil took both Hannah and Sandra to Agra to see TAJ MAHAL, the symbol of love and Red Fort and left for Germany after two days to come again after six months.

18

The honourable Judge of family court of Mumbai, accepted the request of both Anil and Sandra and issued them the divorce document on mutual consent and Anil as per his request, was issued a certificate, indicating that he was now single. This Certificate was a basic requirement of the registrar of marriage in Germany. The final documents were submitted and the permission was granted to both Anil and Hannah to get legally married and remove the tag of cohabitation partners.

Now the romance between Hannah and Anil had met the reality, organizing their wedding had come close to their hearts. They both needed time and effort especially for the required paper work. Anil collected all the documents required and proceeded to registry office. All statutory document precisely needed were;

1. Both the partners must be present in office
2. Both will require birth certificates
3. Both will need Passports to as a document of their residence
4. Certificate of being Single in case one was married earlier.

All these documents along with the legal fees were submitted and authorities verified them. They were then declared married, husband and wife as per local laws. The marriage certificate was issued. After they had taken the vows, they were embarking on the most exciting journey of their lives. There was only one happiness in their life to love and be loved. Hannah always used to say to Anil, "Learn to enjoy every moment of your life and the best thing to hold onto in life is each other."

Anil always put his wife's needs above his own so his love for her always increased. This always kept alive the spirit of romance in their marriage. Hannah had learned that love could make Anil vulnerable, childlike and unable to do what was expected of him. She needed affection and foreplay as well as sex because that was what made her feel loved. Anil sometimes felt or thought that if sex was good, everything would fall into place. Hannah agreed to some extent and said, yes, sex was a sensitive barometer to what's going on all aspects of our lives and relationships.

The first stage after marriage was honeymoon. Both Anil and Hannah ensured that this special day was followed by the most special holiday.

They first started with the breathtaking scenery on a RHINE CRUISE past historical ruins and castles and experienced the magic of moonlit night and starry sky over their this romantic journey. On way they took part in wine tasting directly at the vineyards and learned about wines and wine making. They stayed in a four star Castle Palace Hotel DRESDEN near ELBE river and enjoyed every moment of their stay.

Today "It's our wedding night and two of us wanted to be alone together." "Today as husband and wife, there seems to be more pressure to make this night amazing and to do something 'wow'."

To make this night one out of blue, Anil and Hannah gazed each other, touched each other's arm or hand and stole some kisses. The hotel authorities gave them a special honeymoon suite, well scented and this smell of scent and flowers carried to their brains, emotional centre when they remembered their memories, emotions and moods and also stimulated their senses. They soothed, energized and aroused for need and desire. Anil specially arranged Sandalwood, Lavender and Jasmine scents to increase arousal and sexual desire. Hannah played some light music.

Hannah was wearing a soft silky, pink coloured lingerie. She was looking extra sexy and inviting one. Anil was feeding her strawberries and chocolates. Chocolates contain caffeine and a feel good chemical called PHENYLETHYLAMINE, both of which are good for mood for sex. Anil knowingly arranged these things for his lady love and they had gone for this. Their sexual encounter was not the first one as they had gone for it many times under their cohabitation arrangement but Hannah said that this time their sexual encounter was most exciting and amazing.

Their intimacy always meant a feeling of ease, honesty and emotional closeness, between both of them. Their commitment meant devotion or faithfulness and passion meant an excitement and desire to be together always.

19

After a divorce, Sandra experienced a magnitude of problems in the social arena. She also encountered greater social barriers to dating and remarriage. She was afraid and hesitant to make friends with men because if she did it, she would be assumed as a woman frivolous, immoral and sexually permissive. Sandra also experienced problems with sexual harassment at work place and on a social scene.

It was difficult to leave her husband and expect to accept her destiny. She was standing on a junction where she was not able to decide whether to move on or be like what she was till now. "Happiness is every human's right and why she would only sacrifice her freedom and should think that divorce is a positive change, change for her to live like a normal woman."

"Everyone has a right to live life on his or her terms so why not Sandra?" She thought to herself. Just because she was a divorcee it didn't mean that her sex life had to dry. Sandra was young and had her bodily needs so she was sometimes finding her life entering a second phase of her sexual life.

Yes, the parting ways, social stigma were signaling the end of a meaningful relationship but it was also leading to a new path of sexual self discovery. The only male, not a friend suddenly put her in a weird position. He initiated and she followed practicing her flirting skills at every opportunity. The thrill of meeting him was wonderful and she was enjoying the anticipation as much as active sex. Sex after Sandra's divorce made her feel completely vulnerable at first. It was a long time since a man had really looked at her with passionate eyes. She gave herself a permission to feel good and be a normal woman.

He was a bit younger to her. He had a great smile, a great body, sexy hair and he really knew how to handle a woman. For Sandra, it was a clean slate beginning, the past wiped off. Whether it was out of rebellion revenge, she became a bit more of a sex symbol with excessive desire. She used to openly tell her friends that her sex life after divorce was better than the sex, she had while married. She became extra open and used to reason out for her enhanced and better sex life. According to her, after having sex with only one man for so many years was boring and with someone new was exhilarating that made her feel like a woman again. Each man had his own ways and tricks into the bedroom or in the shower and frankly speaking , there were no strings attached. Every man gave her different pleasure and some feelings of her being a teenager.

Some of them even offered a ton of money and some latest cars. She was no more a simple domestic divorcee but at the same time, she was also not a professional call girl or sophisticated prostitute. She was mostly seen with a male at so many public places like hotels and social clubs.

20

Both Hannah and Anil had a family life full of fun and romance. The fear that after some years their initial spark would die, never proved to be correct as they both worked hard on keeping the romance alive and on continuously growing. The most important part of their happy married life was that they never fought with each other, Anil always respected Hannah and always consulted for any decision however big or small. He heard her seriously and both of them always agreed for a common agreement. He was kind, loving and understanding to his wife. Hannah was also so confident of her husband that she never did any snooping through his phone or computer. They never discussed their past or past mistakes. Hannah never reminded him about his failures but always worked on reinforcing positive vibes and enjoyed every moment of present time together. They maintained strong communication and left nothing unresolved.

Hannah was a typical German wife, very economical and fully domesticated. She was never angry on Anil. She always cared about his moods and thoughts. She was damn good in reading Anil's body language. Their bonding was so deep that the chances of breaking marital confidence was zero. They trusted each other more than anyone in the world. Anil always said "I love you" before going to work which was to convey how much he loved Hannah. He never forgot to send minimum four messages of love and erotic sex to her.

The nights for them were always romantic and scintillating. They were both very regular on bed or any remote corner of their house. For them, sex was more than just sex. Making love with Hannah was very intimate and fun activity. It helped both of them to a strong marriage because of the closeness, they both shared during the act.

Hannah got pregnant within two years of their marriage but their kissing or cuddling never skipped. Anil spent a lot of time with Hannah. Hannah was no less romantic. She always surprised Anil with little gifts as a token of love and respect.

They both adopted each other's friends and families into their lives. Of course Evan was always a priority for Hannah. They were now waiting for Evan to arrive.

A son was born to Hannah. A cute little thing half Indian, half German in looks and skills. Hannah named him Paul Malik.

21

Evan was 11 years now and was to go to 6th Standard. Hannah remembered her plan of admitting him in 6th Standard and she was predecided to put in a boarding school in Sanawar. She talked to Sandra and she came to Mumbai with her son Paul. Anil had some important assignment of Govt. of Germany so he did not make it this time.

Both Hannah and Sandra took morning flight to Chandigarh. They hired a cab from Chandigarh to go to Sanawar. Hannah had zeroed down to this school after comparing best schools in India. Both Sandra and Hannah saw the school, studied their education standard and other curriculum. THE LAWRENCE SCHOOL, Sanawar was established in 1847 by Sir Henry Lawrence and his wife Honoria. The school is situated at a height of 1750 metre and spread over 139 acres in Himachal Pradesh. It is a co-ed boarding school, affiliated to CBSE pattern. There are students of different background, different parts of the sub-continent. It provides an environment for clear air, clean study of subjects and provides avenues to the students for expressing their creativity and skills. In addition to the classroom syllabus, Hannah noticed and informed Sandra that the wards of who is who had studied in this school. People like Omar Abdullah, Captain Amrinder Singh, Maneka Gandhi, Ness Wadia, Saif Ali Khan, Pooja Bedi and PreityZenta were few names. Activities like horse riding and Polo were added facilities.

Hannah didn't think long and admitted Evan in Standard 6th. The huge amount of education and boarding fee was paid by Hannah. Sandra agreed and appreciated the gesture. Evan was to join on June 10 which Sandra would arrange to send.

Both the ladies visited tourist places of Himachal Pradesh and Srinagar.

Hannah went back to Germany after two weeks of stay in India.

22

Sandra's son left to his boarding school at Sanawar with his mother as per his schedule for the first time away from her. She was feeling miserable and the thought now coming to her mind was that Evan didn't need her anymore and she couldn't stop crying. She was too attached to him and it was quite painful to her. But for the fact that each person can't be only one person all the time, she tried to reconcile with the irony of fate. Even Anil had left her. She had to take things in her stride and understood that this was the reality of life.

She thought that she had to detach from Evan as he would be chasing his dreams. She said, "I have to somehow make myself strong and would definitely not feel miserable.

Back home, she engaged herself in her routine things but one thing she was most uncomfortable was the question Evan asked," when would Papa come to stay with us along with Hannah aunty and Paul? She had no answer and Evan didn't insist for the answer. Sandra understood that Evan now knew everything.

Sandra spoke to Hannah and informed her about Evan's reaching THE LAWRENCE SCHOOL, SANAWAR. She couldn't resist telling Hannah about Evan's question and his anxiety. They both were saddened for a while.

23

Sandra was a changed person and was mostly doing things and engaging herself in the activities impetuously. Meeting some unacceptable people with complicity was preposterous which sometimes, some days would definitely get her in ignominy. The money, she was earning from her parlour business was looking like peanuts or like temple alms and she wanted to earn a lot of money irrespective of all ways and means.

Sameer, the only man seen with her all the time introduced her to a network of Call Centre girls, University girls, girls staying in hostels and paying guest accommodation, air hostess and models engaged in sexual activities. This business was operating like an Industry and was changing drastically. It was not that the girls from poor families were forced to prostitution to earn money but girls now were willingly getting into the trade for quick money, fun and entertainment. There was another set of lonely house wives or sex starved women who entered into this sophisticated prostitution. Young girls from rich and affluent families got into this for sheer excitement and adventure. Some women entered in this trade simply because they were bored of one man and wanted to explore Sex with multiple partners.

Sandra was lonely sex starved and Sameer told her that she could earn as much as Rupees One Lac per day making the offer irresistible. So she thought that why marry when you can live in? Sandra was exceptionally beautiful and her language was an added advantage. She soon acquired her customers of high profile businessmen, bureaucrats and top producers and directors of the film world. She had crave for quick money, lavish life and high end cars. By the way Anil and Hannah gifted her the high end BMW on her last birthday.

Sameer became a house hold name for Sandra and was present with her all the time of day. When the neighbors wanted to know about the identity of the man, they were told that he was a driver but for the residents of the society, he was much more than a driver. When they were not satisfied with the answer, the angry residents decided to take the matter in their hands. Over 150 of them confronted Sandra and Sameer and raised the ruckus, Sandra told them that she would change the residence in next 15 days. The matter was also reported to Police. A team from special cell from social was working on specific inputs about a sex racket in Sandra's house. A Policeman was sent as a decoy customer claiming to be a big businessman from South Africa following which the police raided the house. The special team rescued two women, one a Call Centre employee and other a final year student of hotel management institute. Both Sandra and Sameer were taken into Police custody but later released on personal security of Rs.50,000 each.

They shifted their residence in another Colony but the bad name reached before the bad deed. Over there also, identity of Sameer was a big problem. However Sandra always introduced him as her personal driver.

24

Time was moving at its own pace. Sandra was busy in her activities Evan was growing at a much faster pace and had already reached in 12th Standard at the age of 17 years.

Hannah one day while surfing internet noticed a news item of Sandra being arrested and released on bail for some sexual violation and brothel case. She was shocked and disturbed. Hannah after seeing this report felt tired and exhausted. For her, this news was incredibly jarring and it almost turned her world upside down. She called up Anil and waited for Anil to return from office. When Anil came home, she offered him a hot cup of coffee and took him in confidence. She revealed what she saw or internet and showed him also the entire news item. Anil too was shocked and stressed. Traumatic stress for him was a normal reaction to a traumatic event. This news caused intense, confusing and frightening emotions. He entered a state of shock and disbelief. He had fear, sadness, helplessness, guilt, anger and shame. Hannah consoled him and gave him time to heal and also controlled his difficult and volatile emotions.

The immediate thought which came to their minds was to isolate and insulate Evan from reaching even close this news. They both decided to bring Evan to Germany.

Evan's exams for 12th Standard were getting over by end of next month. They had time to prepare the documents for his immigration. Both Hannah and Anil discussed to visit Mumbai and not make Sandra aware of their knowledge of Sandra's activities and her pending legal and police cases.

They only informed Sandra that Evan after passing 12th Standard would need a professional study either in Engineering or Medicine so they would like to take him to Germany and would ensure that he became a qualified professional. They also requested Sandra to shift to Germany along with Evan. She could stay with them and could start her business if she so desired.

After six weeks, Hannah and Anil visited Sandra and wanted to know her answers. Sandra as usual was sharp. She said that it would be difficult for her to move because of the parlour but would agree to send Evan for further studies. She knew that by sending Evan, she would not like to be exposed in Evan's eyes because sooner or later he would come to know about all her illegal and immoral activities.

Evan left with Hannah and Anil with all his certificates and other documents. Sandra hugged him, thanked Hannah and Anil and promised to all three of them to visit Germany after six months.

Evan since beginning was inclined towards Computers. In Germany, Computer Sciences are one of the most desired fields of studies. The country offers terrific employment market even for international students. Hannah got him admitted in the first semester of Computer Science in U.L.M. University. He became a hosteller over there also who could visit Hannah and Anil either on weekends or during vocations. Evan loved Hannah more than his father.

25

Sandra was a free bird now after Evan left for Germany and her desire to own a fleet of all imported cars and to have a house even bigger than the richest man of India became her priority to fulfill and accomplish. Growing up in a small house gifted by Anil, she established a small unit, manufacturing the contraband in Bhiwandi near Mumbai. She soon established marketing contacts with Anjani Rao of Hyderabad and Basavraj of Mangalore. Now she had full-fledged marketing network at Hyderabad, Bengaluru, Goa, Delhi and Jullandhar.

Money started flowing via HAVALA sources. Mumbai soon became a Ganja/Drugs/Narcotics capital of India. Not only that 75% of the terrorists had established connections with this little known place in Mumbai for obvious reasons. She dispatched one consignment of 250 Kg contraband containing Rohypnol, Ketamine to Hyderabad which was noticed by Hyderabad Police and five drug peddlers were arrested by Hyderabad Police and the contraband which was brought by them was seized. All the five, arrested were handed over to the crime branch of Police and after looking into organized drug syndicates operating from Mumbai and also after investigation (THIRD DEGREE), they confessed the source and involvement of Sandra. Hyderabad Police along with Mumbai Police swooped down on Sandra's residence and her manufacturing unit early in the morning and arrested Sandra. She was taken to Charminar Crime Branch Hyderabad for further investigations. Based on the confessional statement of Sandra, the Police seized over 500 Kg contraband valued at Rs. 14 Crores. They also arrested two more employees of this so called Pharmaceutical company.

Hyderabad Police informed that this gang of Sandra and associates had international connections and had supplied huge consignments of these drugs to so many dealers in the past. The most common drug which was manufactured by small scale unit of Sandra in the name of manufacturing cough and cold tablets and capsules were Rohypnol Ketamine the nick name for street drug.

These drugs were used to assist a sexual assault. These drugs are powerful and dangerous. They could easily be mixed in normal drinks without being noticed as they do not have any colour, smell or taste, they affect the victim almost immediately making her weak and confused and unable to refuse sex or defend herself. The victim also doesn't remember what happened white she was drugged.

Sandra was charged under production manufacturing profession, sale purchase, Import & Export, interstate export and use of Psychotropic sub-stances but she was acquitted due to lack of evidence, mishandling evidence and witness being hostile and she was set free after three months.

26

Evan was in final year of Computer Science and he acquired in depth knowledge of Computer Science mainly Software and Hardware development using programming skills to control electronic and mechanical device. He also learnt systems from designing Software or designing with Microprocessors involved in gaming industry.

Evan was also growing to become a fully developed and matured man both physically and mentally. He was turning mighty handsome stud who could steal any girl's thunder. Evan was having an attractive, well-proportioned body with good looks and very cute eyes. He was gracious, generous, graceful and appealing. His dressing style was perfect and that gave him a dynamic personality. Hannah was able to help Evan grow into a caring, confident and responsible man.

Anil was very particular about Evan's growth in the engineering college and hostel. He again reminded Evan that this was going to be best days of his life. His room in the college hostel was the perfect place where he would learn most of his lessons of life from his seniors and classmates. He further advised his son to be regular in final year to maintain at least 90 percent attendance in classes. This would certainly help him to be recognized by the professors to score good internal marks. This was the last time, he would be able to make some good friends. He also advised him to participate in all extra-curricular activities like sports, cultural acts like drama and singing. Evan was explained the importance in taking part in technical events like Techfest and finally to study hard in his final year. He followed his father's advice religiously and started job orientation programmes of Campus interviews. His eyes were focused for a job in either IBM, INTEL or MICROSOFT.

Evan appeared in Campus interviews for all three multinational giants MICROSOFT, IBM & INTEL fully prepared academically and attitude wise and he was picked up by MICROSOFT and was advised to join after his final year results at Munich. He was excited and more than him was Hannah who actually transformed him to face any interview. He called up Hannah and informed her that her efforts had borne fruits. For the first time, he used the word Mom to Hannah. Hannah after hearing the word Mom, was on cloud 9. She congratulated him and asked to come home immediately after final examinations and also advised him to call up dad and inform him. He informed Anil about his selection in Microsoft. Anil was equally excited to hear his son's achievements and asked him to send his acceptance to Microsoft.

Though Evan was happy and proud to have done it, somewhere in the back of his mind, something was bothering him. He called up Hannah late in the night and informed her that he would come down to meet them during this weekend as something was bothering him and he wanted to seek personal discussion. He didn't reveal anything to Hannah in spite of her repeated requests. He only said, "Mom, I would prefer to discuss with you and Dad in person on next Friday evening or Saturday morning. Hannah's anxiety was increasing with each moment but there was no option left but to wait for Evan to reach home. After the dinner they all sat together. Both Hannah and Anil were inquisitive to understand what is bothering Evan. Evan said, "Even though, I am selected by Microsoft and I would have a lucrative job but when I look at the poverty and administrative system failure, lot of corruption etc., my heart weeps for my countrymen. I may not be able to eradicate all the problems but whatever little, I will be doing for my country, would satisfy me." "If you both permit me, I would like to join IAS Cadre and would do a bit for them."

Hannah Evan the life in India would be very difficult, specially when most of studies had been in Germany. I appreciate your feelings for India but give it a second thought.

Evan Mom, I have studied the conditions in India and you have made me strong to face any challenge or hardships in India or elsewhere.

Anil Evan, are you aware that IAS examinations are the toughest in the World.

Evan Yes, Dad, I have seen the syllabus and agree that I would have to study 18 hours a day to prepare for qualifying the written test and personal interviews. I would get through, may be at most in the second attempt.

Anil Do you know that to be eligible to apply the Civil Service Exam, a candidate has to be citizen of India and should have a degree from Central, State Universities of India?

Evan Yes, Dad, I have gone in depth for the eligibility criteria. I am an Indian citizen and my university of Germany is approved by Indian Universities forum. I also know that there are 10 Lakh aspirants every year in India, Nepal and Bhutan.

Hannah Evan, think twice before you take this step. I know, you will be happy to stay with your mother but ambience is absolutely different over there as compared to your atmosphere in Germany.

Evan I am fully aware of your worries Mom and I would like to confirm that I would not stay with my mother. I would go to Delhi straight away from here. I will join one of the best coaching institutes for IAS, for one year, would rent an accommodation in some good area of Delhi. Mom, you would support me financially and morally all the time.

Hannah Yes, Evan, my love and support to you is always unconditional. I am not bothered about your finances but I am actually worried about your stay in India. I will always remain on oxygen.

Anil We will support you but would not like you to meet Sandra. Me and Hannah would visit you twice a year.

Evan Mom, Dad, I am aware why you do not want me to meet Sandra. I am not a kid, I am aware of everything about Sandra. I would never meet her until Hannah tells me. I would not go to that coal mines of Sandra to get even one small mark of black coal. Hannah heaved a sigh of relief and both she and Anil gave him permission to opt out of Microsoft offer and start initiating admission formalities immediately after the final year results. Hannah got a special cake for Evan and they all celebrated the event.

27

Evan reached Delhi along with Hannah and Anil after his final year results were declared. He passed his engineering in first class with respected marks. While he was in final year, he had applied to appear in UPSC examination for IAS examination scheduled to be held after one year. Evan while filling his form, had given his preference for IAS than IPS and then IRS and has selected Delhi cadre in case he got through.

Hannah and Anil arranged a one bedroom flat for him in Hauzkhas area at a monthly rent of Rs.30,000/-. It was air-conditioned apartment, peaceful and quite close to his coaching institute for UPSC SRIRAM IAS Classes, Rajinder Nagar, New Delhi.

Since there was a gap of 10 days before Evan's classes started so Anil suggested to visit Kerala with Hannah and Evan. He planned this visit of Kerala to make Evan and Hannah aware of the natural beauty and rich cultural heritage of this Indian state popularly known as 'Gods own country', situated in between Arabian Sea and Western Ghats, Kerala has 44 rivers, tranquil stretches of Emerald back waters, lush green hill stations, waterfalls, sprawling plantations of tea and spices, Ayurvedic health centres, ancient art forms and exotic cuisine.

They took early morning Jet Airways flight and landed at Cochin. A nice air-conditioned Toyota car was already waiting for them with a local driver. They proceeded towards Munnar which is approx.. 135 Kms or 4 hours drive. The drive was divine. They enjoyed the splendid view of tea gardens. There was absolute green backdrop and waterfalls. On the way they saw spice gardens of Cardamom and other spices. After reaching Munnar, they checked in a five star super deluxe hotel and relaxed for a day. Next day they saw famous Mattupetty dam and did boat drive. Their stay at Munnar was altogether good.

Next day, they drove to Thekkady 110 Kms from Munnar. They visited few waterfalls and Periyar wild life sanctuary. After reaching Thekkady, they had nice local lunch. After lunch, they had gone to elephant Safari, saw Kalari-Payette, a traditional martial art form, Kathakali show. Hannah though initially scared of Ayurveda Massage, enjoyed it totally. Fourth day, they visited Kumarakom and stayed in a houseboat. Though the houseboat cruise was quite enjoyable but overnight stay in the boat was a nightmare due to too much noise of the crew and the mosquitoes.

Their experience at Kovalam sight-seeing was too good. Absolute clean sea water and clean beaches made Hannah happy and she spent a lot of time in Sun-bathing. They happily returned to Delhi after a pleasant trip.

They stayed with Evan for two days and after being satisfied with all arrangements of Evan's stay and food etc. Hannah left with a heavy heart with Anil back to

Germany. Evan assured Hannah, "Mom, I would be just fine, would talk to you regularly and would not meet Sandra."

28

Almost all her friends deserted her company for the negative influence, they had because of her name and acts. Everyone said, "A bad deed is better than the bad name. They all knew that Sandra had troubles with law, drugs and worse and she was always derailing them from their actual goals of life and if they continued, they were also losing their personal finances by continuing with Sandra. They all parted ways from Sandra as the continuance would cost them value, destiny, their image. They never wanted their lives to become a topic of gossips. If they didn't leave her now they would become their own enemies and it would appear to them as if they have been conquered and assimilated by her bad ideas. Finally they all concluded that having a relationship with people like Sandra, the person of questionable character was like playing with a razor blade on one's skin. A bad friend is worse than an enemy.

Once they left Sandra, they all were at peace so they knowingly said Goodbye to her. Now Sandra was left with only one friend, Neeta who was social neglect due to her bad temperament. She was a friend not by choice but by compulsion. This friend was frustrated in life because of odd reasons and they both were complimenting each other like a drowning man catches a straw. The second was the same man who had physical intimacy with Sandra after Anil left. Sandra used to term that man sometimes as a driver and sometime as family friend but the whole world knew that man was a physical need and a support for a possible trouble in public areas. This man was actually like a shadow right from parlour to restaurants and clubs. He wanted to be friendly with all the men, Sandra knew but majority of people never ever wanted to even shake hands with him as they all thought that it was below their dignity to even notice him. For some people, his reputation was that of a pimp or broker. Even Sandra's female friend also always stayed away from him.

29

Evan was working very hard at his coaching institution. The IAS conducted by UPSC is generally the toughest examination in the world. Evan knew it very well. He also knew that for selecting 1000 officers, the number of applicant is approximately ten lacs. Evan had almost one year for preparation so he prepared himself in a disciplined way and focused way with a passion for learning and reading. He worked very hard on analytic and presentation skills along with in-depth knowledge of the subjects. He very systematically prepared for prelims and both the part of written examination. Apart from his normal subjects, he chose Geography as an optional subjects so he concentrated on current events of national and international importance along with their geographical locations. He collected data from the toppers and Google. He went into depth of Indian and World Geography including the latest changes, amendments, boundary rows. He studied Indian Constitution, latest amendments, poverty, economical and social developments of India. He soon acquired knowledge on Environmental changes, Montreal protocol.

He purchased all the relevant books of all possible writers like Mr.Mukherjee for Indian independence,

Our Parliament by Mr.Kashyap, Indian Economy by Mr.Ramesh Singh. He took all print outs of question papers of last ten years with their best possible answers. He also downloaded general study booklets 01, 02, 03, 04, 05, 06, 07, and 08 and learnt them by heart. He cleared his preliminary examinations and made himself ready for the written examination of Paper 1 and Paper 2. Throughout the year, he maintained his cool, attended all the classes and exams with a relaxed mind.

When the results of written examinations were declared, Evan was declared qualified and was placed on 93rd rank. He was very happy that he cleared UPSC in first attempt. He only had a reservation that he was not selected for IAS and in turn he was shortlisted for IPS. When Evan informed Hannah and Anil they were very very happy and proud of their son's achievements and directed him to go for IPS training. He left for his training first to Mussorie and then to Hyderabad for final training.

The training of Evan as an IPS trainee was carried out initially for three months at BSNAA in Mussoorie as a basic and foundation course and for one year, he attended Phase-I training at NPA, Hyderabad. The training involved at Hyderabad was ranging from normal policing to counter insurgency policing in deep and dense jungles. He was trained in study of Criminal Procedure Code CRPC, Indian Penal Code IPC, Indian Evidence Act and various ways of investigations. The other subjects which were covered in the training were;

1. Study of Forensic Medicines

2. Internal Security
3. Ethics and Human Rights
4. Maintenance of Public Peace and Order
5. Information and Communication Technology
6. Physical fitness including Sports, PT and Cross Country Race up to 20 Kms
7. Weapon training including assembling etc. for Revolvers, SLR, 303 Rifles and hand grenades
8. Map reading of areas
9. Rock climbing
10. Swimming

Evan completed his this one year training and then he was sent for advance training in international laws and Police departments of many Indian States.

Finally the day reached when Evan was given posting in Delhi North as DCP, North Crime Branch. Hannah and Anil both attended his final pass out parade and they enjoyed the glory of being Evan's parents. He took charge of North Zone, Delhi in IPS uniform as DCP Crime.

Both Hannah and Anil left for Germany after three months of stay with their son.

30

Sandra's business of supplying drugs and contraband had her popularly known in the circle of political leaders and Mumbai Police. She was able to establish good relations between corrupt Police Officers and greedy Politicians of Maharashtra, U.P., Bihar and Haryana. Over the past two decades, charges and allegations have flown thick and fast over thriving criminal-political nexus in Maharashtra. Several state level politicians had long standing or newly established ties with the Underworld Dons based in different countries.

These Dons used Sandra's charm and their muscle and money power to influence local Politicians to help key development schemes in Mumbai and certain big national or international purchases in Government Sectors and in return these Politicians amassed a big fortune for their poll funding. At one point of time, even Sandra was so powerful that she was able to get some of her own people in public position like Chairman of some standing committees and Police Officers on important and lucrative postings.

With the help of some local Politicians and second and third ranks of the Don, Sandra established her own business links in Pakistan, Afghanistan and few African countries. Money was not a problem at all for her. She started living a lavish life style with so many imported cars, new bungalow purchased and refurbished for Rs.900 Crores. She started attending parties of big celebrities from business world, show business and top ranking Police Officers. The income tax and DRI had their eyes set on her but the secured protection from big bosses was holding them not to act.

With the help of underworld, she was able to get some of her competitors or unwanted elements, eliminated to get her ways in. In Mumbai Police itself, she was able to get close to twenty Police Officers dismissed from service.

She was rich, charming, powerful and extremely busy in her business that she practically lost all contacts with Anil, Hannah and her son from so many years. In fact he didn't ever remember the face of her own son as he had grown so big. She hardly knew that Evan was in India as a senior IPS Officer. Even Hannah had not called her since last 15 years.

31

Sandra's drug mafia and the terrorists in Indian border countries was like a wicked marriage between the two. Globally drug trafficking was not only a criminal issue, not just a health and safety issue, it was a national security issue. Most of the terrorist organizations were being funded through the money earned on drugs and contraband. So far she was not directly dealing with any terror group but her drugs were being used by these groups through some contacts in Middle East. She did not realize that terrorists and traffickers were easily contactable because they had common enemies, the law enforcement and intelligence services.

Sometimes, Sandra was in a dilemma to deal with these agencies due to conflict within her for her patriotic feelings but as drugs knew no ideology, it became difficult for her to come out of this vicious circle. She anticipated death both ways by terrorists or traffickers group or finally by law enforcing agencies. In fact under threat, she lost her territory to these anti-national gangs and she only remained a puppet in their hands. She had no option but to toe their lines. She had nobody to fall upon or take her out of the soup. She trusted her conscience and made up her mind to die because of cross firing between them and her changed heart but she would not do anything to endanger the safety and security of India. She tried to stop her business of drugs but now everything was controlled by Tom (name changed), the central point of contact for terrorists and traffickers. She was absolutely helpless. At times, she tried to flee the country but the vigilant eyes of these terror groups didn't let her move and she was under self-exile. All her movements and calls were put under strict scrutiny. None of her so called friends in the Political and Police circles helped her.

Indian law enforcing agencies with all its intelligence, narcotic policing and military intelligence were working hard to break this nexus and also to break the backbone of these groups by checking and stopping money inflow to them.

32

One unfortunate day when Sandra was there in Srinagar to settle some financial dispute of Rs.50 Crore with one Abdul Raza, a famous drug peddler operating in Jammu and Kashmir, Pakistan and Afghanistan. While she was discussing the issue with Abdul Reza in a remote village of J&K's Shopian district, she had to face a group of terrorist who came to collect some drugs and Rs. 10 Crores from Abdul Reza to create a big strike in Mumbai.

Based on the input from the locals and military intelligence that some militants were hiding in that house, the security forces cordoned off the area but did not fire fearing the civil causalities. Taking advantage of the situation and dark, the militants ran away in those nearby dark bushes and nearby jungle. Sandra also ran away along with Abdul and was saved from sure death. She returned to Mumbai next day without collecting any money from Abdul.

The security forces had called off the night-long operation as the militant holed up in that house escaped. The security forces who entered the house at 9 AM next day, did not find any militant. There was no response to the security forces firing and when the army's paratroopers entered the house, it was empty. The search continued for an hour following which the operational was called off.

The security forces including the army, the J&K launched Police's counter insurgency special operation group and CRPF had a cordon and search operation in Shopian village from house to house after receiving information about the presence of group of militants. Two to three militants were holed up in one residential building which was evacuated by the security forces.

The two sides exchanged gun fire for a couple of hours but security forces suspended the firing to avoid collateral damage. Flood lights were installed, civilians were evacuated unmanned Aerial Vehicles (VAVs) with Cameras were installed. There was resistance from the locals but forces had to clear the area of the militants. The gun fire continued for twelve hours. The militants threw several grenades. Finally the house was blown off by security forces by using grenades and heavy artillery and all three militants were gunned down.

When Sandra watched this encounter live on T.V., she was shaken. She felt sheepish, outrageous and self-hated. She developed some sort of auto phobia. She started hating herself. She stopped manufacturing and dealing in drugs from that day but the stock of drugs already available with her in her manufacturing unit along with raw material was yet to be disposed off.

33

Some senior minister from Delhi called up Sandra and asked her to bring 5 Kg of Ketamine as it was urgently required by his counterpart in Ethiopia. Sandra refused by telling him that she had stopped dealing in drugs. The minister threatened to expose all her dirty deeds to CBI and would invite more trouble. In case you wanted to get rid of these problems and if you wanted my help, then you would be required to make at least this consignment. I would protect you from law enforcing agencies of Maharashtra and Central Govt. agencies. She trusted him and planned to do it once for all and she prepared a consignment of 5 Kg to be delivered to Delhi.

In a major crackdown, sleuths of the Narcotic Control Bureau (NCB) and Anti-Narcotic Cell (ANC) of Delhi Crime Branch led by DCP Evan Malik nabbed five drug peddlers including a woman when they intercepted a truck bearing Maharashtra registration number near Gurgaon entrance at Sohna road and recovered 5 Kg of drugs worth Rs. 2 Crore. The driver Vinay Patil was arrested along with two Peddlers Ashwin Kale and Vinod Khade. The lady was also arrested who landed from Mumbai by an early morning flight and had come to that area to collect the consignment. The name of the woman was not revealed till further investigation as she was suspected to get involved in much bigger crimes.

Acting on specific information that the truck would reach Sohna road before heading to old Delhi market, the officials led by Evan Malik reached the spot a night before to keep a close watch on the movement of the vehicle and the people in that area. The moment the said truck reached at the designated place, there was movement of some suspicious people including one woman. They swooped on the truck and arrested three men and one woman.

On interrogation, the accused men revealed that 5 Kgs of drugs were concealed under the driver's seat in a cavity specially made for this transport. Evan arrested all these accused under section 8(C)rw, 22(C) of NDPS act. Evan Malik revealed the name of the woman arrested to his superiors.

He informed Commissioner of Police, Delhi that the arrested woman, Mrs.Sandra Malik was Ex-wife of my father Mr.Anil Malik and she was my biological mother. I would request you Sir, to hand over this case to some other officer. Mr.Amar Chaudhary, C.P., Delhi transferred this case to Mr.Arvind Malhotra, DCP North Zone, Delhi.

Immediately after this, Evan spoke to his father Anil and Mom Hannah and informed about the arrest of Sandra. Anil in a choked voice asked Evan, the reaction of Sandra, when she was arrested by you, Evan? Evan told him that initially she did not recognize me but after seeing the name plate on my uniform, she knew that she had been arrested by her own son. Dad, she had shown some mixed feelings on her face. First feeling which I could notice was that of irreconcilable type, second, a feeling of being distraught, thirdly, an incredible and unbelievable happiness on her face. May be a thought that she had been arrested by her son. Hannah asked "what did you do then?" I simply arrested her, under relevant sections of law of land and got the case transferred to other Police officer. Hannah said " Evan, I am so proud of you my son." Anil seemed a bit disturbed but soon conciled with the reality. He also appreciated his son's action in Sandra's arrest.

34

Sandra was lodged in Delhi's Tihar jail and her bail application was rejected pending detailed report involving some high profile political leaders. She requested the honourable court to transfer the case to Mumbai jurisdiction as she was a single woman and there was no one to take care of her house and business. The honourable judge of Delhi court accepted her request and transferred her case to Mumbai.

A special court in Mumbai sentenced Sandra to 10 years rigorous imprisonment under the Narcotic Drug and Psychotropic substances (NDPS) Act for trying to smuggle 5 Kgs of drug Ketamine from Mumbai to Delhi. It was proved in the lower court that Sandra was the main accused and others were just couriers. N. K. Sharma, Special Public Prosecutor informed the court that during subsequent investigation and interrogation, the Police found that the drug consignment was manufactured, sourced by her and was to be delivered to a Politician in Delhi. The honourable Judge made it a point to investigate this case against the accused Politician also later.

Sandra and her advocates tried their best to dodge the law via legal loopholes specially in event of Sandra being a woman drug peddler but the Public Prosecutor Sharma and the Delhi Police officer Malhotra made a very tight foolproof case against her.

Arguments and counter arguments were given and all the witnesses were examined. None of the witnesses turned hostile. There were sufficient gaps, repeated charges and inconsistencies in Sandra's statements. The honourable Judge of the lower court found her guilty and awarded her 10 years rigorous imprisonment.

Sandra and her accomplices, convicted by the lower court were again convicted by the high court as the case was watertight for the first time unlike so many such cases in the past where the culprits were acquitted due to legal loopholes and poor investigations/execution by the Police and legal experts.

She was transferred to Yerwada Jail at Pune for the period of her proposed jail term. To encourage living a positive life, Yerwada Jail provided Sandra Creative Art Therapy which helped her in releasing anger, feelings of distress and revenge and of hopelessness. As she was well educated, she was entrusted the work of teaching English to the inmates and also some management skills. All her inmates were respecting her like a true teacher.

She was also entrusted to keep a record of inmates' health and other social needs. Though she was teaching the people the ways of reformation, there was a void in her own life. Concerted efforts were taken by prison authorities and other NGOs to improve her mental health by conducting Yoga and Meditation classes but the improvement was too little and she was mostly quiet and hot focused.

She requested the jail authorities to provide her some stationery as she wanted to pursue writing which was accepted and arrangements were made immediately.

She was mostly seen scribbling something on a writing pad whenever she had time for other than what she was supposed to do as a paid prisoner.

35

Sandra expressed the desire to the Jail Superintendent Mr.SatishKamle to meet Anil, Hannah and Evan at the earliest. Mr.Amit Deshmukh after talking to Anil confirmed that this meeting would be possible after 10 days. It was confirmed by Evan that both Anil and Hannah would visit Mumbai after ten days. As per schedule, Anil, Hannah and Evan reached Yerwada Jail at Pune.

Sandra wanted to meet all three of them separately which was never a problem. The first meeting was between Sandra and Anil. Sandra told Anil that though we were amicably divorced but I always wanted you to remain in my life. She always felt that she was always part of family including Hannah and would always remain in love with all of them. She said, " Yes, I like to talk about sharing too much history not to be in each other's lives any more. I am glad that our divorce doesn't mean the end of knowing each other. I don't think of myself as a very jealous person to Hannah and don't mind her being with you. On the other hand, I feel happy and confident that you and Evan are in safe and loving hands of Hannah, I would remain her fan till my last moments."

Sandra requested Anil to camouflage Hannah and insulate her from all evils and troubles of life. She was in fact the best gifts God had given you. Anil responded, "Sandra I am sad about the end of our relationship but understand it now that at present moment, it was the right thing to do."

Anil confessed that it was a mistake of leaving you alone in Mumbai but certain things normally were controlled by heart not by mind. Yes, Even when romantic relationship didn't work out, deep friendship would abide. Your friendship with me and Hannah would strengthen by being supportive during the times to come. "Hannah sees your sadness as an indication of her true character that she is capable of real love and would never wipe you from her heart even if she is away from you."

Sandra thought to herself that she was very fortunate that instead of hate anger and betrayal Anil carried that regret and retained his love for his previous marriage. This was an excellent thing in form of a grown up gentleman Evan.

SHE HAD NO REGRETS NOW

Evan said that in his experience it is common. My father's first wife was a good woman. "I felt like confronting you many times Mom but I checked myself. To me, Mom, you are an honourable person and is valued the most. I don't want to go into the history of our entire relationship and also do not want to raise fingers on you or Dad but whatever has happened to me or could have happened to me, you both are responsible." I thank Mom Hannah who preserved my childhood, developed my youth and guided me to be what I am today." Mom, let bygones be bygones but for me money and revenge are irrelevant. I would never lose my mind on anyone of them."

I have loved you as my biological mother but to protect you to avoid law of land, my contribution would be zero as I think if " I do it for you, I will have to do it for all the wrong people."

"Mom, you are wrong and you are suffering." After the expiry of your jail terms, I would personally come with Dad and Hannah Mom to take you Home. This is your son's promise to his Mom."

Hannah told Sandra that it was an isolated feeling and I could try my best to avoid your feelings of discouragement and resentment. We both would try to leave our past behind. It was a mixture of disgust and fondness for each other. These bits and pieces of the history of our relationship would surface every now and then and we both would deal with them gently and firmly. Evan would be an unbreakable link between both of us. I have brought up your son in such a way that he would never deviate from the call of his conscience. He would prove to be the best human being of we two Moms and none of us would play a second fiddle to him. We would now wait for you till you are kept here under the law of land. It would take a lot of strength to overcome feelings and develop trust.

We would meet again, Sandra. Tears rolled down from their eyes. YOU WOULD BE MY BEST FRIEND.

They all left Sandra in Yerwada Jail and returned to Mumbai. They all were not their usual selves.

Both Anil and Hannah left for Germany the next day and Evan after overcoming his emotions too resumed his work at Delhi.

36

Sandra expressed her desire to the honourable court through Superintendent of Jail to grant her permission to donate 25% of her property to STAIRS, empowering youth an NGO against DRUGS and 75% equally to Anil, Hannah and Evan. In her application to the court, she said that she had seen miseries of life and she wanted to help this organization working for rehabilitation of drug affected people.

She was now ready to WILL her property to STAIRS, Anil, Hannah and Evan and in turn required the honourable court to show no leniency in providing any relief to her jail life. She also confessed that there was no way to atone for her crimes but she believed that a profound benefit to society could come from her circumstances. The honourable court was quite considerate and allowed her WILL items in TOTO. The Jail authorities also provided her an expert to draft her WILL in absence of Anil and Hannah but called Evan to be present during the write up of Sandra's WILL.

The entire property was divided as desired by Sandra. Her Parlour and SPA was converted into a rehabilitation centre for drug affected patients and was being looked after by Hannah.

Evan, Anil and Hannah donated their share of property to an NGO called DNA that could benefit single mothers and their dependent children to lead a peaceful, decent life and also a healthy social life without hunger and poverty.

Part of money was also used for single mothers to educate a girl child. They all of three wanted to see smile on their faces. Their aim was to make a project which was designed to provide the daughters of single mothers a safe and loving environment to study in and complete their mother's wishes. It included their, the basic training in Computer skills as well as hone their interest in a dancing, meditation, art and more.

They all did it in style and dignity.

Anil forgot his guilt and Hannah forgot her busy schedule in this project. Evan made himself the messiah of all poor, downtrodden and helpless people around him.

37

Sandra had everything going for happy life and peaceful mind ever since she met her family and after writing her WILL, then one day severe depression turned her world topsy-turvy. The same day when she was coming back from a hospital after medical check-up, she felt a sudden jolt and started palpitating. She came back to jail and she just shut herself from the world. Sandra entered into a Disconnection Syndrome. She never wanted to see anybody, hated everyone and was struggling physically and mentally. To her everything seemed unreal and everyone around negative. She started breathing heavily, the Doctor was summoned and some antidepressant pills were administered and she appeared to be better now.

Sandra was frequently suffering from extreme mood swings as noticed by Jail Doctor and authorities. She was in extreme anger range or vengeful feelings, and in strong feelings of guilt or shame and on top of all, a feeling of loneliness.

She sometimes expressed a deep love for her family but also a compelling desire to relieve the burden from her head, heart and soul. The pain of existence often became too much for bearing and the thought came to her mind that a pervasive sense of suffering as well as the belief that escape from it is hopeless.

Finally one night Sandra committed suicide by cutting/slitting her wrist by using a piece of broken glass on the Jail itself. On her suicide note she wrote, "I was never like that, I was simple, busy in my own world and work. I loved him, he left me for another woman. What was my fault? Yes, I chose it in retaliation, not by choice. I never loved anyone after Anil, all which was construed as love, was just lust, need of the body.

Subsequently, it was all reactions to action and circumstances necessities and compulsions, fear, duress, threat.

Even my Son, my own blood didn't love me. It wasn't his fault, after all who could touch that infectious and cancerous body of mine to spread the mental agony and mental disease.

I have loved, appreciated and kept Hannah on my top most esteem as she had been a better mother than me to my son Evan.

Though I have grudge against Anil but at the end of my breath, I pardon him. Evan would prove to be a wonderful son to Hannah. SANDRA BECAME A BODY AND SCISSORS BECAME SIEZURE.

OTHER PUBLISHED BOOK BY DEVI RAGHUVANSHI

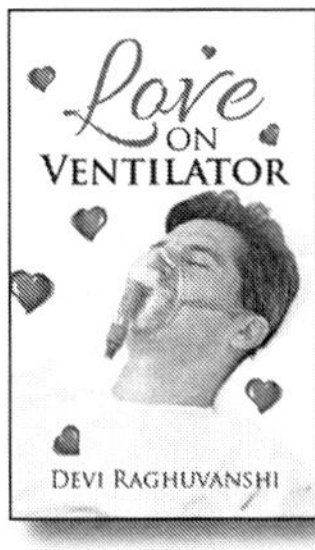

Love on Ventilator

From epic poetry to Hollywood blockbusters, we hear that true love happens only once in a lifetime. But Ajit has a second chance. The inevitable is just around the corner in Love on Ventilator.

Love Triology, Who to Complain

When Ajit suffers an injury that keeps him from fathering children, he refuses to marry his girlfriend, Sudha, and instead marries the woman he saved in the accident that caused his injury.

It's Ok to Fall in Love Again

Ravi is thrust into another adventure as he leaves his dark past. Where will this lead him? And will there be a time when he can fall in love once more?

The Son Rose from the West

Follow an enthralling and evocative chronicling of a love story that will not only entertain but also enrich every reader's view on romance and relationships. Witness an odd yet refreshing take on love and life with Devi Raghuvanshi's The Son Rose from the West.

Mohini The Tigress

Mohini was the beauty like la belle dame sans merci. She was the victim of circumstances. She was gangraped. She not only avenged her rape but also ensured a death fear in the society that many rapes were thwarted because of the fear. She generated in the minds of rapists, murderers. She was the TIGRESS as the word defines.

Other Titles by MyBooks Publication

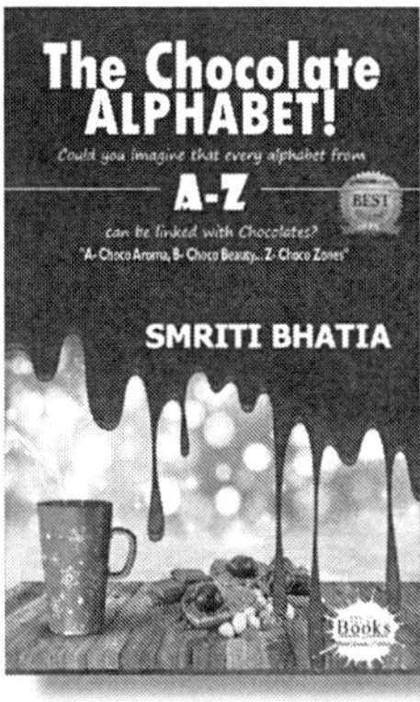

(कविता संग्रह)
दोस्ती

INDIAN
INSTITUTE
OF
IDIOTS
APPROVED
ABHINAV SENGAR

एहसासों के पन्ने
कविता संग्रह
आदर्श राठौर

Torn Pages
by
ANKIT KUMAR

A Month Of my Life, Just like..
CUP OF COFFEE
Anushka Jain

BETRAYALS
deep from the core
ARPIT KULSHRESTHA

SORRY
I WAS WRONG
RISHIKUMAR THAKUR

Behind
the Veil
Qasim Kashmiri

In the Canopy of Life
जीवन की छाँव में
Ayushi Singh

ज़िंदगानियाँ
भाग - १
राहुल जैन
(राही)

INFINITE LOVE
(A Collection of Poems)
Bhuwiii's
Poetry

Tales
from My Soul
AMRITA DEV BURMAN

अनकही
यादें
भरत मिश्रा

SUCCESS
MANTRA
LIFE LESSONS FOR EVERY ONE
SANTOSH KUMAR

THOUGHTS
&
PERCEPTIONS
VIKRAM JOSHI

इंद्रधनुष
काव्य-संग्रह
विनीता ए कुमार

दूब
हनुमंत किशोर

स्वप्नसाक्षी
राकेश कुमार नन्दा

ANUURAG
अनुराग
ज्योति तिवारी

LIFE IS A JOURNEY
a collection of short-stories
Edited & Compiled by
Saba Firdous

CharacterLess
Nishant Srivastava
CharacterLess Nishant Srivastava

MOHINI
the TIGRESS
Devi Raghuvanshi

एहसासों का
आशियाना
Edited & Compiled By:
Saba Shahid

FOREVER,
A LIE
Edited & compiled by Carlos Luis

गुलशन

Dr. Surjeet Singh 'Kunjai'
Sweet & Sour
Tastes in Human Life

Beyond words
And
Between the lines
Naren

THE HIMALAYAN SWAMI
an eerie story
Mike Rana

THE RETRIBUTION
Shankar Kashyap

Love & Romance
Jyotirmaya Thakur

GLIMPSE OF LIFE
Arpan Ghosh
Sneha Pandey

Rhythmic Ocean
SIDDHARTH KUMAR
Books

EPISTLES
...a book of letters
Conceptualized &Edited by
Rituraj Anand

PREGNANCY GUIDE
HOME REMEDIES FOR PREGNANCY
KSHAMA RAO

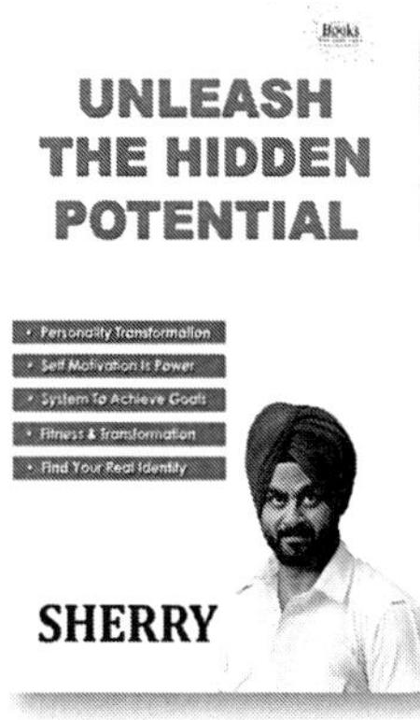
UNLEASH THE HIDDEN POTENTIAL
Personality Transformation
Self Motivation Is Power
System To Achieve Goals
Fitness & Transformation
Find Your Real Identity
SHERRY

HAPPINESS
Building Strong Relationship
Rajan Mehra

अनुराग
ANUURAG
Jyoti Tiwari

When
The Desert
Blooms
Dr. Arvind

ART
Heart of the World
Dr. Aarti Makkar

एक आतंकवादी की
आत्मकथा
अशोक बाघ

LOVE LOST
IN TRANSIT
Devi Raghuvanshi

सेहर
वर्षा धामा

अच्छी सी कोई बात
Achchi si koii Baat
اچھی سی کوئی بات
शमीम अब्बास

लम्हा
लम्हा
प्रशांत सिंह